AuthorHouse™
1663 Liberty Drive
Bloomington, IN 47403
www.authorhouse.com
Phone: 1 (800) 839-8640

Because of the dynamic nature of the Internet, any web addresses or
links contained in this book may have changed since publication and may
no longer be valid. The views expressed in this work are solely those
of the author and do not necessarily reflect the views of the publisher,
and the publisher hereby disclaims any responsibility for them.

ISBN: 978-1-7283-2544-6 (sc)
ISBN: 978-1-7283-2545-3 (e)

Library of Congress Control Number: 2019912972

This book is printed on acid-free paper.

Print information available on the last page.

Published by AuthorHouse 09/30/2019

authorHOUSE®

BZZZ Z Zz
BZZ Z Z Zz
BZZ Z Z Zz
BZ Z Z Z Zz

# BIJOU
## Chases
a
## Bumble Bee

Wendy Worden

Illustrated by VECTOR FAMILY

There is nothing I like better than napping in the sun.

What is that noise that dares to disturb me during my nap?

What is that?

Excuse me... You do NOT want to swat at the bumble bee.

Who are you?

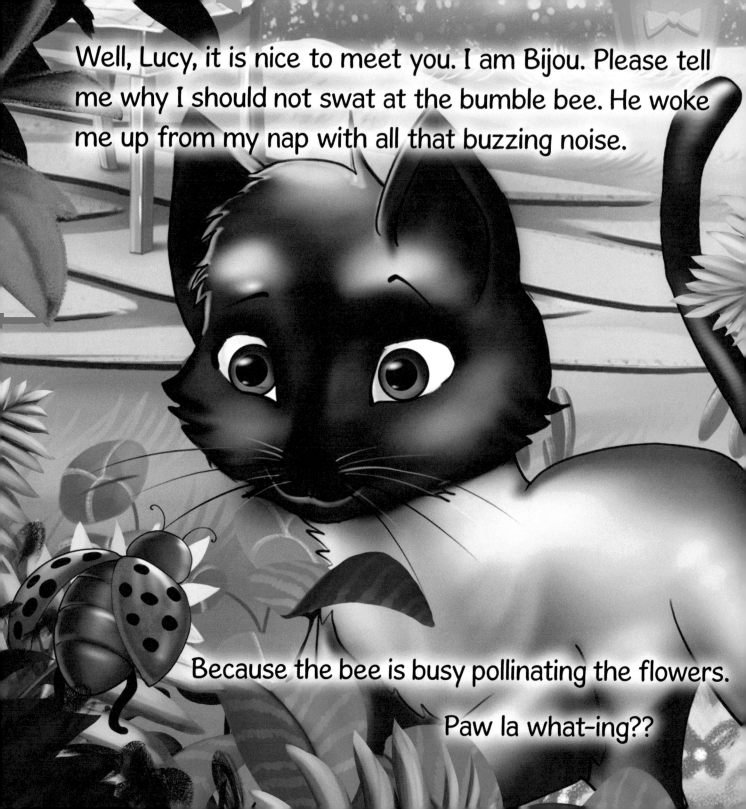

Well, Lucy, it is nice to meet you. I am Bijou. Please tell me why I should not swat at the bumble bee. He woke me up from my nap with all that buzzing noise.

Because the bee is busy pollinating the flowers.

Paw la what-ing??

Poll-in-ating. If he doesn't do that, the plants won't grow and multiply. Bees go from one flower to the next spreading pollen which allows flowers to grow. If there were no bees, we wouldn't have flowers.

Huh? You seem pretty smart.

How'd you learn that Lucy?

Oh, I know a lot of things because I hang around watching and listening to everything around me.

Do you "paw-lin-ate", Lucy?

Oh no, I help to protect the plants by eating the insects that destroy the plants.

I like to eat bugs too, Lucy.

But don't worry, I won't eat you. You're too pretty....for a bug!

But this bee is annoying Lucy, and he needs to go away so I can finish my nap.

Bijou, stop swatting at him because he will sting you
and it hurts to be stung by a bee.

Well, he's flying away now.  I guess I showed him who's boss around here!

Ha...Ha...Ha...

Why are you laughing at me Lucy?

Because you didn't chase him away. It was time for him to move on to other flowers.

Lucy, would you like to stick around for a while? You're so smart and I'm...well...NOT...I could learn a lot from you, and we could have some great adventures together.

That sounds like fun Bijou.  Where should we go first?

First? First, I need to finish my nap.

Printed in the United States
By Bookmasters